MR. MEN
ADVENTURE IN
EGYPT

Original concept by
Roger Hargreaves

Written and illustrated by
Adam Hargreaves

EGMONT

Little Miss Splendid was on holiday in Egypt with her friends. They were travelling down the river Nile to see the Pharaohs' treasures.

As they sailed down the Nile they came to the great temple at Luxor.

Little Miss Splendid looked enviously at the giant statues at the entrance to the temple.

She would have liked a giant statue of herself.

A giant statue of Queen Splendid of the Nile!

Inside the temple, the columns and walls were covered in ancient Egyptian writing.

Mr Nosey could not understand the hieroglyphics.

"I wonder what that says?" he asked.

"That says, Big Nose!" laughed Little Miss Trouble.

Outside the temple they found some camels and one, who looked as grumpy as Mr Grumpy, ate Little Miss Splendid's hat.

"That's my best hat!" cried Little Miss Splendid.

Poor Little Miss Splendid had to wear her second best hat.

She was not very happy.

In fact, she looked as unhappy as Mr Grumpy.

The camel, on the other hand, was much happier after its snack.

They climbed aboard the camels and rode into the desert under a blazing sun.

"It's too hot," complained Mr Grumpy. "And these camels are very uncomfortable to ride!"

Little Miss Splendid had to agree as she swayed backwards and forwards on top of her camel.

Camels were definitely not her idea of luxury.

They travelled on across the sand dunes until they saw an amazing sight in the distance.

It was a pyramid.

The tomb of a Pharaoh.

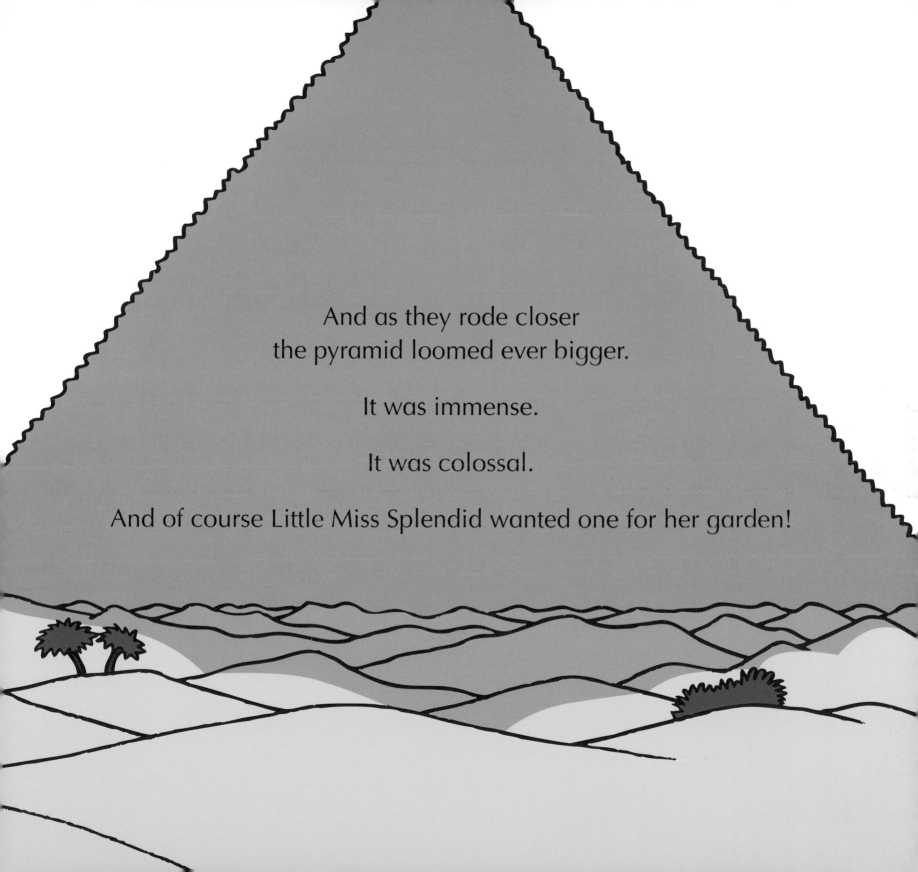

And as they rode closer
the pyramid loomed ever bigger.

It was immense.

It was colossal.

And of course Little Miss Splendid wanted one for her garden!

In fact that was not all that Little Miss Splendid wanted for her garden.

They rode past the Sphinx and she thought that a Sphinx would look very grand on her driveway.

"Or maybe two of them," she said, "either side of my gate."

"Why not three?" muttered Mr Grumpy.

It was dark and cool inside the pyramid.

"It's too cold," complained Mr Grumpy, as they followed a very long winding passageway up and down countless steps and around many twisting turns.

It made Mr Worry very nervous.

Finally they reached the chamber in the centre of the pyramid where they found a sarcophagus and in the sarcophagus was a mummy.

"Look at all those bandages," said Little Miss Somersault. "Mummies must have been even more accident-prone than Mr Bump!"

Through another passageway they discovered a room full
of the Pharaoh's treasure.

It was piled high all along the walls.

Little Miss Splendid gazed at the glowing
golden furniture and ornaments.

"Now that gives me an idea,"
she said.

There were even more treasures at the back of the room where Little Miss Splendid found the Pharaoh's crowns and headdresses.

Which of course she had to try on.

She sat on the Pharaoh's golden throne.

"Now, this is the life, this is the real me," she announced.

"You look ridiculous," said Mr Grumpy.

Little Miss Splendid ignored him and enjoyed her daydream until it was time to leave, but nobody could remember the way out.

"Oh my goodness," shrieked Mr Worry. "We're trapped! We'll never get out! We're doomed!"

"Mr Noisy could shout for help," suggested Little Miss Somersault.

So Mr Noisy shouted at the top of his very, very loud voice.

"HELP!"

But all it produced was a terrible, deafening echo that rolled and reverberated around the chamber.

HELP! HELP! HELP!

"What's this?" asked Little Miss Tiny, picking up what looked like a bandage.

"I think that belongs to me," said Mr Bump.

And it was indeed Mr Bump's bandage.

It was then that he realised that nearly all his bandages had come off.

"If we follow Mr Bump's trail of bandages then perhaps we can find our way out," suggested Little Miss Tiny.

And she was right.

It was a very relieved Mr Worry who finally emerged from the pyramid.

"I think it's time to go home," he said. "That's enough adventure for me!"

"Me too," agreed Mr Grumpy, looking the happiest he had all trip.

And Little Miss Splendid could not wait to get home and change her hat.

Can you guess what was the first thing that Little Miss Splendid did when she got home?

After putting on a new hat, that is.

She rang her builder.

And ordered a pyramid!

And a statue, two Sphinxes and a modest-sized temple.

But no camels!